ASH BAR

PRESENTS...

Little ASH

Perfect Match!

BOOK 1

Written by
JASMIN McGAUGHEY

Illustrated by
JADE GOODWIN

HarperCollins*Children'sBooks*

Chapter One

Hi there! My name is Ashleigh.
I'm seven years old. My big sisters,
Ali and Sara, call me Ash. In fact,
almost everyone does!

Today is the first day of Year
Two. It's a **big day** and I'm a little
worried. Not about school. I love

school! Plus, I already know that my **best friend**, James, will be in my class. No, I'm actually worried because this week I have to pick the **sport** I'm going to play on the weekends for the whole entire year. But I don't know what to choose!

I'm relieved to see James at the school gates. When I see James, I forget my worries. So I tell him my **best joke** while we walk to our classroom with my mum.

'Why did the kangaroo cross the road?' I ask.

'I don't know, Ash. Why did the **kangaroo** cross the road?' he asks. James is always super interested in my jokes.

'Um …'

'Oh no. Have you forgotten the punchline again?'

That's the trouble with the jokes I tell. I often forget the **funny** bit. 'Never mind!'

'Now, Ash,' Mum says. We are at the Year Two classroom door. 'Don't forget to think about what sport you want to play this year. Okay?'

Nervous butterflies go wild in my tummy. 'Okay, Mum!'

She gives me a hug. Her hugs are the **best**. They are soft and comfy. I could fall asleep in Mum's hug.

After she leaves, James and I wait outside our classroom door.

'I heard your mum ask what sport you want to play this year,' he says. 'Will you choose softball again?'

I shake my head. 'No way. I've tried netball, softball, karate, *and* gymnastics. And they were fun, but they didn't give me that **tingling**

feeling in my hands and feet. You know that feeling? The one that tells you that you **love** what you're doing.'

James nods, but then our new teacher arrives before he can answer.

'Hello class! My name is Mr Howard. Come inside!'

Mr Howard is **super tall**. He is almost as tall as the door! He gives us a big smile and tells us to sit on the floor.

'I need your help,' I say to James as we sit down together. 'Or I won't be able to pick a sport by the end of this week.'

'Got it,' he says.

James is the best, best friend I could ever ask for. But even *with*

James's help, I am nervous. What if I can't find a sport that I absolutely love? What if I get stuck with a sport that I absolutely hate … for a **WHOLE YEAR?!**

Chapter Two

The next day, James and I start Project Find-A-Sport-That-Ash-Loves.

'Okay,' James tells me at morning tea, 'you have got to **trust** me.'

He gives me a handball and puts me in a square inside a four-square grid that is marked out on the concrete beneath the undercover area outside of our classroom. James also stands in a square, and there are two other players from our class in the other two squares,

Noah and Riley. There is a line
of people waiting to compete.

'Ready?' he asks.

'Ready!'

The game starts off slow. Noah
serves and the ball bounces into

James's square. James carefully uses his hand to hit it into Riley's square. Riley hits it into mine. And carefully I hit it to James.

'Okay. I can do this!' I say to myself.

The game starts to go **faster** and **faster**. But I'm pretty good. One time, Noah doesn't hit the ball before the second bounce and he gets out first, and then James misses a wide shot. So then it's just me versus Riley.

I hit the ball hard and Riley runs to hit it back.

Quickly, I look down at my hands. There is no tingling feeling in my fingers or my toes. No buzzing feeling under my skin.

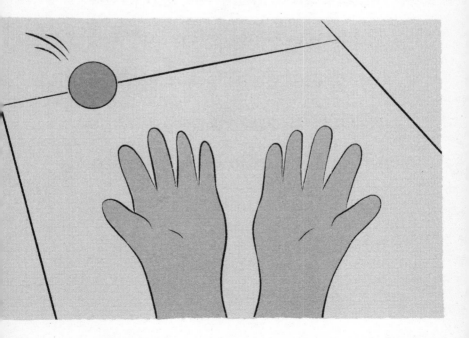

Nothing! I **don't** love this game.

Handball isn't for me.

'Watch out, Ash!' James calls

out.

The ball is spinning toward me.

I have fast reflexes though. My

hand slaps against the rubber ball

and it goes flying!

'Woah!' we all say at once.

The ball **zooms** across the sky.

James points to a bird flying

above us and shouts, 'It's going to

hit that bird!'

My tummy is in knots as I
watch the ball get close to the
flying bird … and miss.

'**Phew!**' I say.

The bird gives us a **mad** look
and flaps away.

'That was a close one,' James says.

Now the ball is **caught** high up in the pine tree out the front of our classroom.

'How about we try a different sport?' I ask.

'Good idea.' James nods his head.

Chapter Three

The next day at lunchtime, James and I ask Mr Howard for some chalk.

'What's the chalk for?' he asks.

'It's for a game of **hopscotch**, Mr Howard!' I say.

'Do you want to play?' James asks our teacher.

Mr Howard shakes his head. 'No thank you,' he says. But he finds us some white chalk to draw with on the cement. 'Here you go.

Be careful,' he says, 'and don't make a **mess!**'

I take the chalk as James and I say together, 'We will not make a mess, Mr Howard!'

'James and I always clean up after ourselves,' I add.

We go outside and James draws the hopscotch outline on the cement path near the sandpit. 'I will go first,' he says.

I stand with my hands on my hips and watch. James **hops** on one

foot. Then he **jumps** on two feet.
He lands perfectly in each square
and then returns back to the start.

Now it is my turn.

I do exactly as he did, and I
move **fast**. In a few seconds, I'm
already standing back at the start.

'Too easy!' I shout.

Next, James throws a rock, and it lands in one of the squares. 'Don't hop in the square with the rock. Then you have to pick up the rock without falling over.'

James goes first. Except, when he bends down and tries to **balance** on one foot as he reaches to pick up the rock, he **falls!**

'Oh no,' he says. 'If you make it, Ash, you win.'

I roll my shoulders. I jump up
and down to loosen my leg muscles.
I throw the rock into a square.
I hop forward once. I hop forward
twice. I hop forward three times
and then jump with two feet.
I balance on one leg and reach
down and grab the rock.

I land on the last spot and lift
my hands into the air. 'I **won!**'
I say.

'Congratulations, Ash,' says
James. 'Is this your **sport**?'

'Even though I won, and it was fun, I don't feel like hopscotch is my favourite game. There are **no tingles**,' I say. 'Can we try something else?'

'I have an idea,' James says. 'It's a **secret** and **magnificent** game that I came up with! We will play it at lunchtime tomorrow, okay?'

'Okay!'

Chapter Four

It's lunchtime on Thursday, and
James has assembled most of
our class to play his **secret** and
magnificent game. We stand
in the grassy area in-between
the Year One and Year Two
playgrounds and the classrooms.

'This game is called **Imagination-ball!**' James shouts so everyone can hear. 'We have to get into two teams and the first team to make it across all the equipment in the playgrounds and back to the classroom before the end of lunchtime wins.'

'What are the rules?' I ask.

'The **bark** is **lava**, and you have to hold the **imaginary ball** above your head!' James says.

We split the class into two teams. I'm the leader of one team. James is the leader of the other team. I bounce on my toes and raise my hands to hold the imaginary ball. I am very **excited** about Imagination-ball.

'On your marks, get set, go!' James shouts.

My team and I **rush** to the Year Two playground. We have to go up the slide and across the balancing bar, up the ladder and down the pole to pass this playground. James's team has run straight to the Year One playground.

My team and I move **quickly**. We help each other up the ladder and I give a hand to Noah as he wobbles on the balancing bar.

Then we go to the Year One playground, and before I know it, we're through it. We run over to the last playground in the game. My team is **hot** on James's **heels**. Which means we are close to running past him. This final playground is huge and is mostly used by the big kids. We swing across the monkey bars. We hop and jump over the lava ground that's really just woodchips. And then we get to the bottom of the hill at the **SAME TIME!**

'First team up to the classroom wins!' James shouts.

'All aboard!' I shout. The other kids on my team run behind me, and everyone puts their hands on the shoulders of the person in front, so we make one big line. I am the leader. James does the same next to me.

'**Brum, brum!**' James says. '**Go!**'

I run as fast as I can up the hill and toward the classroom with the

imaginary ball above my head.
The hands on my shoulders are
heavy. They make it much harder
to run. But I keep going.

'**Never give up!**' I yell to my
team, and to myself.

I am running very fast and

so is James. In fact, we might be
running too fast ...

Ahead, I can see Mr Howard
stepping out of the classroom. He is
holding a tray of paint containers.
The containers are full of **bright
red paint**.

'Oh no!' I shout. I can't stop in time.

The person behind me lets go and I feel my legs **whirling** in the air.

BAM!

James and I run straight into Mr Howard.

The paint flies up into the sky as all three of us fall to the ground with a loud **THUD**.

There is red rain.

All three of us are covered in lots and lots and **LOTS** of red paint.

Chapter Five

Mr Howard wipes red paint from his eyes and then hands me and James a tissue each. The paint is **everywhere**. It's in my hair, under my nails and is soaking my socks.

We are standing next to Mr Howard's desk in our classroom.

We. Are. In. Big. Trouble.

'What were you two doing?'
Mr Howard asks. He flicks some
more red paint from his face. A
droplet flies onto a nearby desk.

'Playing Imagination-ball!'
James says. 'It's a great game.'

'You would love it, Mr Howard,' I add. 'James created it.'

'While that is very clever, you have made quite a big mess,' says Mr Howard.

I **squirm**. I don't like getting in trouble.

'You are going to have to clean up the paint,' continues Mr Howard. He gives us a bucket of water and cloths and points to the classroom door where most of the red paint spilled.

We go over and start work.
James tries wiping the door, except
the paint only spreads further.

'What a **failure** today was,'
James says.

'It's okay, James,' I say. 'I didn't
love hopscotch …'

'And your handball was
terrible,' James adds.

'Do you mean **terribly
fabulous**?' I ask.

'Nope.' James shakes his head.
'It means you nearly **hit** a bird and

lost the ball! That is the **opposite** of fabulous.'

I grumble at him. I'm scrubbing really hard at the ground that has been stained with red paint.

'Imagination-ball was fun,' I admit. 'But I don't think anybody

else knows that game. I probably can't play it as a sport on weekends.'

My shoulders are heavy, but now there are no hands weighing them down. I am feeling a little bit **sad**.

What will I do now? What if I **never** find a **sport** that makes me **happy**?

Chapter Six

James comes over to my house in the afternoon and we go to the backyard to play.

'What do you want to do?' James asks.

'Let me show you my **favourite** made-up game, James. I have been playing it since I was five years old!' I say.

I find the squash racquet and tennis ball and go to the brick wall in the backyard. I hit the ball against the wall. Before it shoots off behind me, I hit it again with the racquet.

It's called a **volley** to hit the ball before it touches the ground.

I'm really good at it.

'Wow, Ash!' James says. He starts jumping up and down on

his toes, very fast. He does that when he's excited.

Mum and Dad come outside and so do my big sisters.

'What's going on?' Mum asks.

'Look at Ash go!' James says.

I hit the ball again and again. Everyone does a **big cheer** every time I strike the ball back toward the wall without letting it touch the ground.

'Look at her foot work!' Dad says.

'Look at her arm muscles!' my sister Ali says.

After a few minutes I'm really sweaty so I take a break. I have a **big smile** on my face and my heart is pumping hard.

'That was so much fun,' I say.

Dad disappears inside and comes back with a different racquet. It's a bigger shape.

'This is a tennis racquet,' he tells me. 'Here, have a go.'

I take the racquet from him.

It's heavier but **feels good** to hold. Mum shows me how to hold it properly. Dad shows me how to bounce the ball and hit it.

I wipe the sweat from my forehead. I don't want sweat to drip into my eyes.

'Remember to take a **deep breath!**' Sara says.

I take a deep breath and bounce the ball. My racquet hits the ball and I move just the way Mum and Dad showed me. The ball bounces back and I hit it again!

I feel a **buzzing** in my hands and feet. Almost like I could **fly!**

'Have you ever thought about playing tennis?' Dad asks me.

'We could sign you up this weekend,' Mum suggests.

I look at James and he smiles.

'Did we do it?' James asks. 'Have we found your next sport?'

I smile too. 'I think we have!'

Dad finds another tennis racquet. Ali and Sara set up some sheets as a net. Dad and I hit the

ball to each other over the sheet. Mum and James cheer us on.

'I can't wait to start playing tennis this year!' I say after hitting the ball over the net again.

I'm happy. I have found the sport that I **absolutely love**.

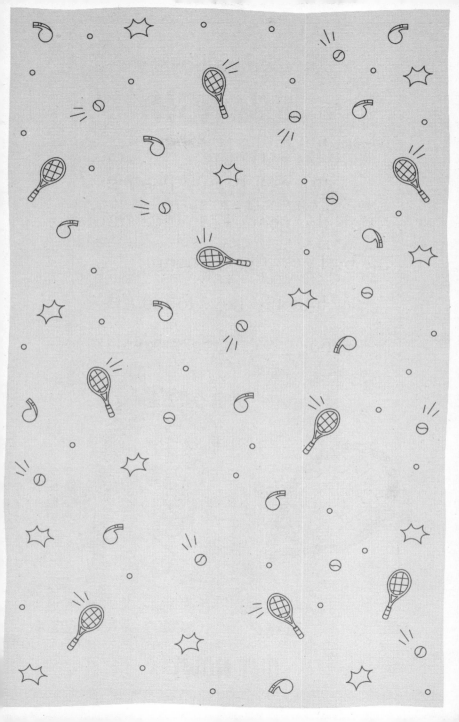

Are you enjoying Little ASH?

Read the next book in the series, *Friendship Fix-it!*

Ash can't wait to play tennis with the big kids at school today! But when James's school project breaks, Ash has to decide whether to help her friend fix his project at lunchtime or play the game she loves. What will she do?

BOOK 1

BOOK 2

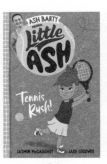
BOOK 3

BOOK 4

OUT NOW!